Daisy Fitzpatrick and her WORRIES

For Nellie and Arthur.

With enormous thanks to my Mum and Dad, without whose expertise, love and guidance, this book would not have been possible.

And to Jo for his untiring patience and calm.

First published in 2022 by Ragged Bears Ltd
www.ragged-bears.co.uk
ISBN: 9781857144895
Text & illustration copyright © Nancy Carroll 2022
Moral rights asserted

All rights reserved. No part of this publication may be reproduced, stored in or introduced into a retrieval system, or transmitted in any form, or by any means, (electronic, mechanical, photocopying, recording or otherwise) without prior written permission of the publisher.
Any person who does any unauthorized act in relation to this publication may be liable to criminal prosecution and civil claims for damages.

A CIP catalogue record for this book is available from the British Library

Printed in China using sustainably sourced paper

Daisy Fitzpatrick and her Worries

Written and Illustrated by Nancy Carroll

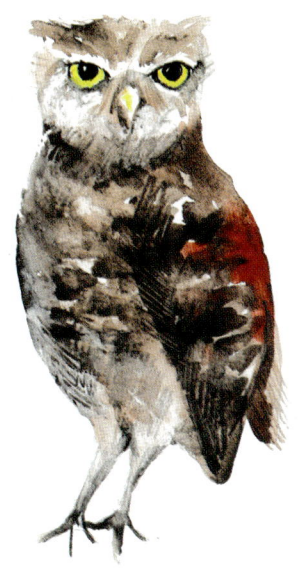

Ragged Bears

1
Daisy Fitzpatrick didn't love bees
Page 6

2
Daisy Fitzpatrick was worried by heights
Page 10

3
Daisy Fitzpatrick was scared of the dark
Page 16

4
Daisy Fitzpatrick wasn't fond of the sea
Page 20

5
Daisy Fitzpatrick didn't like spinach
Page 26

6
Daisy Fitzpatrick didn't like storms
Page 32

7
Daisy Fitzpatrick was scared of dying
Page 38

8
Daisy Fitzpatrick hated crossing the road
Page 44

9
Daisy Fitzpatrick sometimes got angry
Page 48

10
Daisy Fitzpatrick was scared on her own
Page 52

11
Daisy Fitzpatrick had trouble at school
Page 56

12
Daisy Fitzpatrick's Dad had moved out
Page 60

1

Daisy Fitzpatrick didn't love bees,
or clusters of flies
that hover near trees.
She would leap up and down
if they buzzed too near,
shouting and jumping,
'til the coast was clear.
They didn't buzz louder
and they didn't shout back,
but Daisy thought shouting
the best form of attack.
She didn't love wasps,
ants, spiders or worms.
She felt itchy and twitchy,
and they made Daisy squirm.

Moths were too flappy,
mosquitoes too keen,
slugs were too gooey
and beetles looked mean.
When Daisy wrote down
all the insects she hated,
her list over spilled
with fears she'd created.
Then Daisy's Gran Flo
said about bees,
"they're really important,
as important as trees!
They help plants to grow,
they move pollen from flowers,
they're too busy to sting you,
making honey for hours!"
Gran said "worms are ok
and birds like to eat them.
They look after the soil,
and that's why we need them.
The big flies and small flies,
often called gnats,

they're lunch and breakfast
for the birds and the bats.
Like moths and spiders
and worms of all lengths.
And some spider's venom
has medical strengths;
the stuff in their sting
can help us with pain.
That's how spiders and bees
help form our food chain.
We are all connected
and need help to survive;
the world needs it's food chain,
for all life forms to thrive.
Sometimes they're scary,
and sometimes they bite,
and it's totally normal
they give you a fright.
But try to remember
you're bigger than them,
and they're all part of
Nature's perfect system.

2

Daisy Fitzpatrick was worried by heights.
Looking down from a bridge
made her tummy twist tight.
Fairground rides
weren't really much fun.
She took a deep breath
wondering why she had come.
Each rickety whizz,
and leaping drop,
her eyes stayed shut
'til the final flop.
Stairs she could see through,
climbing trees that were tall,
lifts with big windows,
were no fun at all.

And flying in planes,
it was hard not to wonder,
how this great metal bird,
could cope with thunder?
All wind and weather
must be stronger up high?
How then is it safe?
How can planes fly?
So Daisy decided
to search for some reading,
some books to explain
and stop fears impeding
on adventures and trips.
She found some great facts
and discovered some tips.
"It's really common to fear,
looking down from up high.
But height's just a measurement
on a map of the sky.
Every tall building,
each plane and each bridge,
has teams of great builders
for each bolt and ridge.

I imagine how birds feel,
their wings keep them free,
to travel from danger,
across miles of sea.
Like birds, it's planes wings
that keep them so high.

Wings force the air down,
which holds planes in the sky.
An upward force, called 'lift',
overcomes the plane's weight,
and the engine helps speed,
making sure we're not late.
It's crazy but true,
planes are safer than cars!
For over one hundred years,
we've reached for the stars.
Back in 1903,
the Wright brothers first flew.
Just for 12 seconds,
but that's when they knew;
our world could look different
with this science of flight.
The journeys we'd make
with the magic of height.
So when I look down,
I'll try not to despair,
but think of Orville and Wilbur,
the Wright brothers pair.

And the builders and thinkers
who want me to see
the astonishing views
of the land, sky and sea.
They remind us we're small
and nature's so wide,
but how lucky are we
to be part of this ride.
Engineering and flying
are really amazing,
I'll try to stop worrying
and spend more time gazing".

3

Daisy Fitzpatrick was scared of the dark.
"Try not to get worried"
her mum would remark.
"There'll be sunshine at breakfast,
it will all be alright".
But Daisy was struggling
with no lights on all night.
"Dark seems so hasty
To eat up the light,
I can't be alone
in feeling this fright?
Noises seem louder
Every pipe pings
Each door and stair creaks
and the windy night sings

Daisy tried happy dreaming,
She tried to start snoring,
but her scariest thoughts
emerged without warning.
Then Daisy's Gran Flo,
said about night,
"there's lots that's not scary,
the dark's really alright.
We need total darkness
for our brains to take stock.
when humans evolved
the sun was our clock.
Light keeps our minds active,
so dark suits us best,
to deepen our sleep,
and get proper rest.
Just think of the animals
that sleep through our day.
The dark is their daytime,
their nocturnal play.
The aardvarks and foxes,
owls, badgers and bats;
the dark is their blanket;

their safe habitat.
Our sun is amazing,
it's our heat and our light.
But each day the Earth spins
so somewhere it's night.
As we have our breakfast,
Australia's bedtime's begun,
as our bit of the Earth
is facing the sun.
And when you feel scared,
you've five senses not one.
you can smell, taste, touch and listen,
the dark could be fun!"
"Thanks Gran" said Daisy,
"I'll try that tonight,
And remember those things,
When I turn out the light".

4

Daisy Fitzpatrick wasn't fond of the sea.
"It's too big and uncertain,
and frankly, scary.
The water's so deep,
so dangerous and wild.
Just miles of blue
not safe for a child.
"There may be fierce fish,
sharks or sea snails?
Small finned and slimy,
with multiple tails?
I do want to try,
to be brave and just splash.
I just feel too wobbly,
to give it a bash",

Then a lifeguard called Jo
wandering by,
saw the look on her face
so stopped and asked why?
Jo said, "understanding's the key.
about safety and tides,
about currents and dangers
of different seasides.

But the water's so great
for our bodies and minds,
all those vitamins and minerals
of so many kinds.
It heals eczema and cuts,
it helps colds and flu,
it helps our blood and with stress!
Such great things it can do!
It's inspired adventures and poems
of pirates and whales,
sea battles and sailors,
who've passed down their tales.
It's 70%
of our brilliant earth.

It's hard to imagine
all those waves, sea and surf!
And scientists are still learning,
as nature's so clever!
Studying oceans and climates;
how it changes our weather.
They draw maps of sea beds,
study sea creatures,
to discover the magic
of deep water's features.
The sea can be dangerous
and waves can get high,
but they're things we can learn
to help get us by.
There are flags on the beaches;
yellow, green, red and black;
each one is a signal,
where to swim or keep back.

If you're not a strong swimmer,
it's best to beware,
but we lifeguards are trained
for when there's a scare.
We'll jump in and protect you,
swim you to land.
So lookout for the life guards,
we'll give you a hand.
"Thanks Jo" said Daisy,
"I'll dip my toes in,
the sea's so much more
than just to swim in"
Jo said "don't worry,
it's good to be cautious,
but if you're careful and ready,
the sea's really gorgeous"

5

Daisy Fitzpatrick didn't like spinach,
Or broccoli, or greens,
They were too hard to finish.
"lettuce is soggy,
Beans are too long,
Peas are too fiddly,
And sprouts really pong.
Carrots are too orange,
mushrooms just weird,
cucumber too watery
and kale should be feared.
Corn is quite messy
and mashed, roasted or chips,
potatoes are fine,
but better with dips".

Daisy's limited diet
made her Mum frown.
All veg was an effort.
So she sat Daisy down.
Mum said "let's start again,
all veg is great,
you've got it all wrong,
there's nothing to hate.
If we find the right dish,
you'll get all your vits.
We'll make it so tasty,
you won't leave a bit.
Let's try spinach and cheese
In a thin pastry pie,
and broccoli roasted,
now that's worth a try.
Sweet honey dressing
on thinly sliced Lettuce
makes a simple side salad
much less of a menace.
Beans are great
in a salad too

and cooked in a curry
or cooked in a stew.
Peas in fish pie
or mixed with steamed rice.
Cabbage in coleslaw
or soup is quite nice.

Garlicky mushrooms
fried and on toast,
stuffed with cheese,
or baked with a roast.
Carrots grated in sarnies,
or in carrot cake.
Corn frittatas
are easy to make.
Let's follow some recipes,
For taste sensations
that will hopefully end
your 'no-veg' fixations!

"Thanks Mum" said Daisy,
"I'd love to start baking"
Mum said "It's good
to help with the making.
You'll want to try more
once you've chopped, stirred and fried.
When you're full of good stuff,
you'll be glad that you tried".

6

Daisy Fitzpatrick didn't like storms
Or thunder or lightning
rumbling 'til dawn.
They gave Daisy the shivers,
particularly at night.
Even counting between bolts
couldn't stave off her fright.
Each second between bolts
meant miles away,
But the crackling sky
had something to say.
Furious clouds
churned by furious winds,
Bashing at trees,
and knocking over our bins.

Daisy's windows would rattle,
And she'd hide from the noise,
seeking comfort and calm
by hugging her toys.
Then Daisy's friend Stan,
said about storms,
"Like all crazy weather,
in the hot, cold or warm,
it existed before we did.
Sand, rain and snowstorms
have always appeared,
like tornados and hurricanes,
they've always been feared.
There are so many types
of storms and lightning;
understanding them a bit
may make them less frightening.
And knowing that experts,
with sensors and books,
satellites and radars,
who know where to look,
can warn us, inform us,
protect and prepare

for violent wet wind bursts;
so we don't get a scare.
They're called Meteorologists.
They measure all weather;
air pressure and wind speeds,
they're all super clever
they predict all the changes,
old patterns and new.
When the clouds will be dark,
or the sky cloudless blue.
Lightning is electricity
hotter than our sun.
Darting down from the clouds
where it's sparks first begun.
It makes a hole called a channel,

as it strikes through the sky,
as the channel collapses,
thunder's loud gurgling cry,
that crackling clap,
is the noise that we hear.
We'll always be warned
when the storm gets severe.
As our planet gets hotter,
as our climate is changing,
there may be more rainstorms
so we should be engaging
with protecting our planet.
Up cycle, recycle, cycle don't drive,
do all that we can
to help our earth thrive.
"Thanks Stan" said Daisy,
"All this science is brill,
Understanding each noise
makes it more of a thrill.
I'll try not to be scared
but watch storms in wonder,
and remember we're lucky
we understand thunder"

7

Daisy Fitzpatrick was scared of dying.
Life ending was shocking,
she just felt like crying;
with questions and rage,
wishing she knew less.
Like the days before now,
when she thought it endless.
Mum tried to explain,
we all struggle with why.
That it's just a deep sleep
and we all have to die.
But still overwhelmed,
by this idea of an end,
with no hearing or senses,
that we don't always mend.

She asked "where do we go?
Can we really not see?
Can we not say goodbye?
or keep memory?
And dead's a small word
for such big thing.
How do our bodies
just stop working?"
Then Daisy's Gran Flo
said about death,
"It's all part of life.
In our every breath,
are tiny particles,
ancient people breathed out,
that exist in our air
still floating about.
So, wherever we go,
whatever we believe,

our breath makes sure
that we never leave.
There are lots of ways
to understand and prepare.
Different thoughts and beliefs,
journeys and prayer.
They've thought it all through
for thousands of years,
about this life that we know
before an end that sparks fears.
Some people believe
in life after death.
That our souls journey up,
once we take our last breath.
That they'll be with their God,
In a paradise
or high up in heaven
which sounds very nice.
Some people believe
a cycle of rebirth,
leads one life to another,
back here on earth.

That our 'karma'
or how we act in this life,
affects our next time;
if it's joy-filled or strife.
We spend our whole lives
working out what we feel.
We worship and read
and question what's real.
But if we come back,
or wherever we go,
I think mostly it's calm
and there's people we know.
Take your time to find out
what it is that you think,
but, let's guzzle life up,
like the yummiest drink;
make lots of memories,
love, laugh and smile,
and with any luck
we'll be here for a while".

"Thanks Gran" said Daisy.
"I feel less scared than before".
"That's cool" said Flo
"What are Grans for?".

8

Daisy Fitzpatrick hated crossing the road,
She knew all the rules,
but the way people drove,
the speed of the cars,
the tales she'd heard,
made crossing alone
seem frankly absurd.
Sometimes at corners
fast cars would appear
from seemingly nowhere,
igniting her fear.
"If I can't see them,
and they can't see me,
why risk stepping out,
with no guarentee"?

Then Daisy discovered
The Green Cross Code.
"I think this might help me
start crossing the road.
It's great for remembering
6 basic things,
which work really well
for careful crossings.
First find a safe place
to cross in plain view,
of speed hungry cars
not watching for you.
Stand on the pavement
near the kerb side,

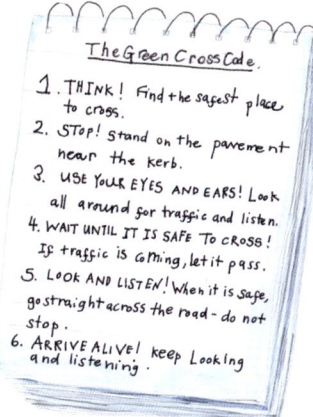

The Green Cross Code.
1. THINK! Find the safest place to cross.
2. STOP! Stand on the pavement near the kerb.
3. USE YOUR EYES AND EARS! Look all around for traffic and listen.
4. WAIT UNTIL IT IS SAFE TO CROSS! If traffic is coming, let it pass.
5. LOOK AND LISTEN! When it is safe, go straight across the road - do not stop.
6. ARRIVE ALIVE! Keep looking and listening.

no toes in the road,
but you don't want to hide!
Use your eyes and your ears,
listen for engines and wheels
never stop looking!
just keep your eyes peeled.
Wait 'til it's safe.
It's not good to run,
this is no time to hurry,
the moment will come.
Looking and listening;
Never stop doing those.
With every new crossing
my confidence grows.
Always looking and listening,
I can now cross alone,
I still prefer it with Mum,
but I can on my own.
It's all a bit daunting
and normal to doubt,
but things have got easier,
Now I've tried this code out!

9

Daisy Fitzpatrick sometimes got angry.
Her nostrils would flare
and her arms went all gangly.
Often forgetting
what started it all;
upset and reasons
in a tight little ball.
Daisy felt dreadful,
The second it finished.
Full of sorrow and tears,
her temper diminished.
As quick as it grew,
Her anger passed by.
Then hot and confused
she would mostly just cry.

She knew it was loud,
she wished she saw sense
before all the tears
before she felt tense.
Some of her friends
rarely got narky,
not even angry,
just saddened and snarky.
So Daisy wrote down
some thoughts about rage,
"I really do hope
this eases with age?
But I think it's important
and a normal emotion.
All humans must feel it?
This internal commotion?
Maybe it's better
if I start to feel grisly,
to walk away for a bit
and avoid any misery?
Slowly calm down
and ask myself why,
work my thoughts out,

let time pass by?
Then when I'm ready
to explain what's not fair,
I might say how I feel
with less heat and despair.
Anger and sadness
are, on the whole,
surprising and sudden
and hard to control.
But whatever we feel,
we need to find words
to express all our thoughts,
however absurd.
There's always a reason
so I'll look for the why.
Take a deep breath
and let out a big sigh.
It might be tricky at first,
but I'll try to keep going.
Talking's the key
to keep it all flowing.

10

Daisy Fitzpatrick was scared on her own.
With no one about,
she felt very alone.
She didn't mind bath time,
although not for too long,
and the loo was ok,
it helped singing a song.
But going upstairs
when the landing was dark
and no one was there,
wasn't fun to embark.
And somewhere unknown,
she suddenly found,
she felt a bit scared
and heard her heart pound.

Daisy longed to be close
to people and light;
rushing towards them,
legs wobbly with fright.
Then Daisy's Gran Flo
said not to worry,
"take your time, turn the light on,
there's no need to hurry.
You're never alone,
the world's full and busy.
If you breathe in and out
you'll avoid all this tizzy.
Breathing's the way
to calm yourself down,
Don't hold your breath,
and try not to frown.
Hear the noises around you,
not the fears in your head.

Let birds, cars and people
fill your ears up instead.
All the hubbub and chirping
that rumbles around us,
the wind in the trees,

all the life that surrounds us.
Smile to yourself,
there's no need to fear,
You're brilliant and brave
and everyone's near.
We all get wobbly,
whatever we say,
it's normal to fear stuff,
at night time or day.
But alone is never
really alone,
its just a short walk
'til you're not on your own".

11

Daisy Fitzpatrick had trouble at school.
Some kids in her class
had called her a fool.
They mocked her red hair,
and laughed when she'd slip.
Put bags in her path
to make sure she'd trip.
They'd conjure new names
only they found amusing,
and behaved in a way
that was really confusing.
These kids had been nice,
they had been her group
But now each lonely day,
saw her confidence droop.

Daisy felt sure
she wasn't the cause,
but their constant abuse
had given her pause.
She'd started to worry
"What if they're right?"
trying her best
to be strong and polite.
Then one day without knowing
how, when or why,
she found a new strength,
and gave smiling a try.
As she smiled in response
she suddenly saw
the light in their eyes
sparkled no more.
Their joy in their jokes,
had stolen her light.
But stealing it back,
let her light shine bright.
"These bullies are thieves,
They lack their own light.
They seek out light keepers

so they feel alright.
They fill each dark corner
of their sad empty tummy,
snatching my joy
and pretending they're funny'.
They continued to pester
and mock for a while,
but their jaunts had lost power
with Daisy's new smile.
Though it's not always easy
when you feel lost and lonely,
to hold onto your light,
to smile can feel phoney.
But it's much the best way
so all light thieves know,
to find their own joy,
so their light can grow.
Daisy now gently
looked forward to each day
She could tackle her worries,
and smile, come what may.

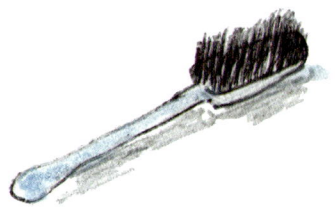

12

Daisy Fitzpatrick's Dad had moved out.
Her Mum and her Dad
just used to shout.
So, now there was quiet
where the tension once sat,
and all of Dad's things
filled a tiny new flat.
On Wednesdays and Fridays
Daisy stayed with her Dad.
They did lovely stuff,
but she still felt just sad.
Her Mum tried to explain
in the simplest way,
The complications of marriage,
and whatever we say

we always love you.
You're the light of our life,
And you're nothing to do
with the anger and strife.
Some days were OK,
She forgot for a while,
Her tummy would settle,
She'd laugh and she'd smile.
Then a thought filled her head
Is it Mum or Dad's night?
Her smile got distracted
and her body felt tight.
She wanted to shout,
or run, or just cry,
To be on her own,
and not have to lie.
Then Daisy's Gran Flo
Said about marriage,
'When Mums and Dads fight,
it all feels so savage.
In all the noise
is confusion and fear,
Pushing loved ones away

when you just want them near,
To hold and to squeeze,
to say that you're sorry.
To end all the rows
and stop all the worry.
But sometimes it's ok
to reach a mutual end,
To regrow apart,
calm down and mend.
You grew from their love
and together makes sense.
That's why parting's so hard,
so gruesome and tense.
But the reality is
parting happens a lot.
Nearly half of all marriages
reach a full stop.
Grown up love is not simple.
And life can be tricky.
Our parents can change
Situations get sticky.
I know you feel lonely
I know you feel lost,

But not talking or shouting
may come at a cost.
Your Mum and Dad love you
to the moon and back,
That love is your home.
It's that you should pack,
in your overnight bag,
with your pjs and brush.
When you start to feel wobbly,
just stop and don't rush.
Remember the love
and the new happy days,
without tension and fighting,
and finding new ways
Of being and travelling
and decorating your room.
It might not feel ok,
but I know it will soon.
'Thanks Gran', said Daisy,
'I'm feeling less sad,
Maybe two bedrooms
isn't so bad.'

Corn Frittatas

Ingredients

You will need a non-stick muffin tin
1 cup (160g) tinned or defrosted from frozen sweetcorn
½ cup (60g) grated cheese
4 eggs
100ml milk
2 tablespoons of chopped flat leaf parsley
salt and pepper

Method

1. Preheat oven to 180c. Lightly grease 6 holes of a non-stick muffin tin.
2. Divide corn between the 6 holes of the muffin tin. Then top the corn evenly with all the grated cheese.
3. Whisk the eggs and milk together. Stir in the chopped parsley and season with salt and pepper. Then pour the mixture into the 6 holes of the muffin tin, on top of the corn and cheese.
4. Bake for 15 mins until light golden brown and set. Cool for 5 minutes, then transfer to plates and serve.

Tip: They taste really yummy served with tomato salad.

Carrot Cake Muffins

Ingredients

You will need a non-stick muffin tin and 12 cup cake cases.
3 eggs
½ cup of greek yoghurt
½ cup of maple syrup
¼ cup milk
1 teaspoon of vanilla extract
2 carrots grated
1½ cups of wholemeal or plain flour
1¾ teaspoons of baking powder
1½ teaspoons of ground cinnamon
1 cup (200g) light cream cheese
½ cup (100g) icing sugar
1 cup of chopped walnuts
(optional - for sprinkling on top of the cream cheese icing).

Method

1. Preheat oven to 175c. Put 12 cup cake cases into the 12 hole non-stick muffin tin.
2. In a large mixing bowl, whisk the eggs until light and fluffy in consistency.
3. Add the greek yoghurt and whisk until the mixture is light and fluffy again.
4. Add the maple syrup, milk and vanilla extract and mix until smooth.
5. Now add the grated carrots, flour, baking powder and cinnamon. Fold in all the ingredients until totally mixed together.
6. Divide the batter in to the 12 cup cake cases.
7. Bake for 20 minutes until muffins have risen and set completely.
8. Remove from oven and allow to cool.

9. Meanwhile, you can make the cream cheese icing by mixing together the cream cheese and the icing sugar until you get a light frosting texture. Once the muffins have cooled, using a teaspoon, ice each muffin generously. As an optional extra, you could then sprinkle the icing with the chopped walnuts. Then enjoy your carrot cake muffins!

Notes and useful links

1.

Bees are important pollinators. This means they move pollen from the male part of one flower to the female part of another flower. There are numerous pollinators including honeybees, bumblebees, ants, flies and moths, amongst others. This essential pollination allows our flowers and food crops to thrive, which means it helps sustain humans. It also supports our wild plants that allow our wildlife to survive. Yet our bees need our help. Pesticides, climate change, disease and the development of land that was once woods and meadows, have seen a number of bumblebee species decline dramatically. If you would like to know more, help the bees or plant a bee garden, contact Bumblebee Conservation Trust at www.bumblebeeconsevation.org.

   The food chain shows us how plants and animals get their energy. It is a cycle that starts with a producer, for example, leaves and flowers, that make their own energy. The producer is followed, in the food chain, by the consumer. The consumer survives by eating the producer, for example a grasshopper. Humans are the consumers at the top of the food chain.

Spider venom contains a huge variety strong and useful peptides. Peptides are things that exist in all of us. They help with the structure of our bodies, for example, our skin, tissue and muscles. Scientists have discovered that for 300 million years spiders have developed these peptides, and they believe they can help humans with cancer, strokes, epilepsy, pain and all sorts of illnesses. They are discovering new and brilliant ways to create medicine from within the natural world, all the time.

2.

Fear of heights is a common fright at all ages. It is a totally natural extension to our normal instinct to steer clear of danger. Like many fears it can be combated by a gentle exposure to situations that trigger those fears, to slowly stretch the boundaries of your comfort zone. With help, we can retrain our reactions to distinguish between our fears and genuine danger.

The American brothers, Orville and Wilbur Wright invented, built and flew the first 'heavier-than-air', motor operated aircraft. It was called 'the Wright flyer'. They are known as aircraft pioneers. A pioneer is someone who opens up new areas of thought or research. On December 17th 1903, they flew 37 meters in 12 seconds. The brothers went on to invent aircraft control and steering systems for fixed wing aircraft that are still used today.

3.

Nocturnal means relating to or occurring in the night. Nocturnal animals are active during the night.

The dark is a magical and powerful thing. An International Dark Sky Places Program was founded in 2001. This was to encourage communities, parks and protected areas around the world to preserve and protect dark sky sites. A night sky without artificial light is vital to the proper functioning of natural ecosystems. Artificial light affects predator-prey relationships, the migration patterns of animals, insects and birds, and sleep-wake cycles. The sleep-wake cycle is known as circadian rhythms.

Artificial light can affect these rhythms, which means our restorative processes are interrupted, i.e. the process of our bodies recharging and taking care of themselves. To find out more about dark sky parks, visit www.nationalparks.uk

4.

The RNLI, or Royal National Lifeboat Institution, provides a 24 hour rescue service in the UK and Ireland. Their lifeguards protect the beaches and their lifeboats help people in trouble at sea. They have saved over 143,100 lives since 1824. They also provide essential safety knowledge for anyone going out to sea or visiting the coast. Visit www.rnli.org for safety information and where to find your nearest lifeguarded beach.

5.

The natural goodness and energy we get from fresh fruit and vegetables, including Vitamin C, Vitamin A, Fibre and Potassium, all help our bodies develop, stay well, active and ready for anything. Even the Gladiators of Ancient Rome were mostly vegetarian, but eating large quantities of beans and barley. After their training and fighting they drank a special drink make from plant ashes to help their bodies recover.

6.

Meteorologists are scientists who use maths and their knowledge about weather patterns, to prepare daily weather forecasts. They are not the weather people we see on the television or hear on the radio, but meteorologists will pass their information to them.

    Lightning is an electrical current. When the ground is hot it heats the air above it. This warm air rises. As it rises, the water vapour cools and forms a cloud. As the hot air continues to rise, the cloud gets bigger and bigger. At the top of the cloud, the water temperature is below freezing and the water vapour turns to ice. Now the cloud is a thunder cloud. The bits of ice in the air, move around and bump into each other. These collisions help build an electrical charge. Once the charge is strong enough, electrical sparks start to happen. This is usually within the cloud, but sometimes between the cloud and the ground.

Our world's climate has been changing since the beginning of time, and it always will. Since the 1950's, however, our climate's temperature has risen dramatically. This is known as Global Warming. Scientists have recorded the polar ice caps melting, the oceans warming up and sea levels rising.
These changes effect the weather, the seasons, our coastlines, the animals and wildlife that need certain temperatures to survive and many other factors.
There is still so much we can do to slow down that process and protect the future of the planet.
For more information on climate change and what we can do to help, there are many websites and charities available.

7.
The word 'karma' literally means 'action'. It refers to a cycle of cause and effect. This means that what happens to a person, happens because they caused it with their actions. However, it applies to all living creatures. It is a very important part of many different religions such as Buddhism and Hinduism.

8.

The Green Cross Code was started in 1970 by the National Road Safety Committee. It was developed to help everyone cross the road safely, especially children. If you would like to know more visit www.roadwise.co.uk.

9.

Many people go through times in their life when they feel more angry or sad than normal. Learning to deal with those times is something we can ask for help with. Anger is a normal and healthy emotion at every age, but there are steps we can take towards feeling calmer. Talking about your feelings is a great place to start.

10.

Focusing on your breathing and listening to the noises around you are two of the principles of Mindfulness. Mindfulness is a type of meditation intended to help us all with reducing stress and relaxing our bodies and minds. There are many books about Mindfulness for children available, as well as information and exercises online.

11.

Bullying affects over 1 million young people every year. It exists everywhere and comes in many forms; but it is never ok to be bullied. It isn't always easy to talk about, but there is always someone who can help. There are many charities available to offer support, information and advice for victims of bullying, or parents of victims.

12.

Divorce and separation are part of life. For children, however, the process of understanding, accepting and change can be difficult and worrying. Talking, listening, loving and reassuring, all help with navigating those changes. Support for children and parents is available from many charities and websites.